A Tall Tale

AA Published by AA Publishing.

AA Publishing is a trading name of
Automobile Association Developments Limited,
Fanum House, Basing View, Basingstoke, Hampshire RG21 4EA.
Registered number 1878835

A CIP catalogue record for this book is available from The British Library

ISBN 0-7495-4700-6
978-0-7495-4700-4
A02616

Printed and bound in China.

A Tall Tale

Written by Michelle Hogg

"Patrolman Pete! Patrolman Pete! Can you hear me?"

Rita at the call centre was trying to contact Pete.

It was a hot summer's day and Rita's phone hadn't stopped ringing as people asked for help to fix their cars. Today, all the cars had broken down on the same road.

"What could be happening?" cried Rita.

"We're ready to roll, Rita!" Pete replied.

"Where are we going?" asked a voice from the passenger seat. It was Trevor the Toolbox – he was always ready for action!

"Hold on, Trevor," said Pete to the excited toolbox. "We must wait for Rita to tell us!"

Pete and Trevor put on their seatbelts and listened to Rita tell them the way. Then Pete started the engine and he, Trevor and Stan the Van set off.

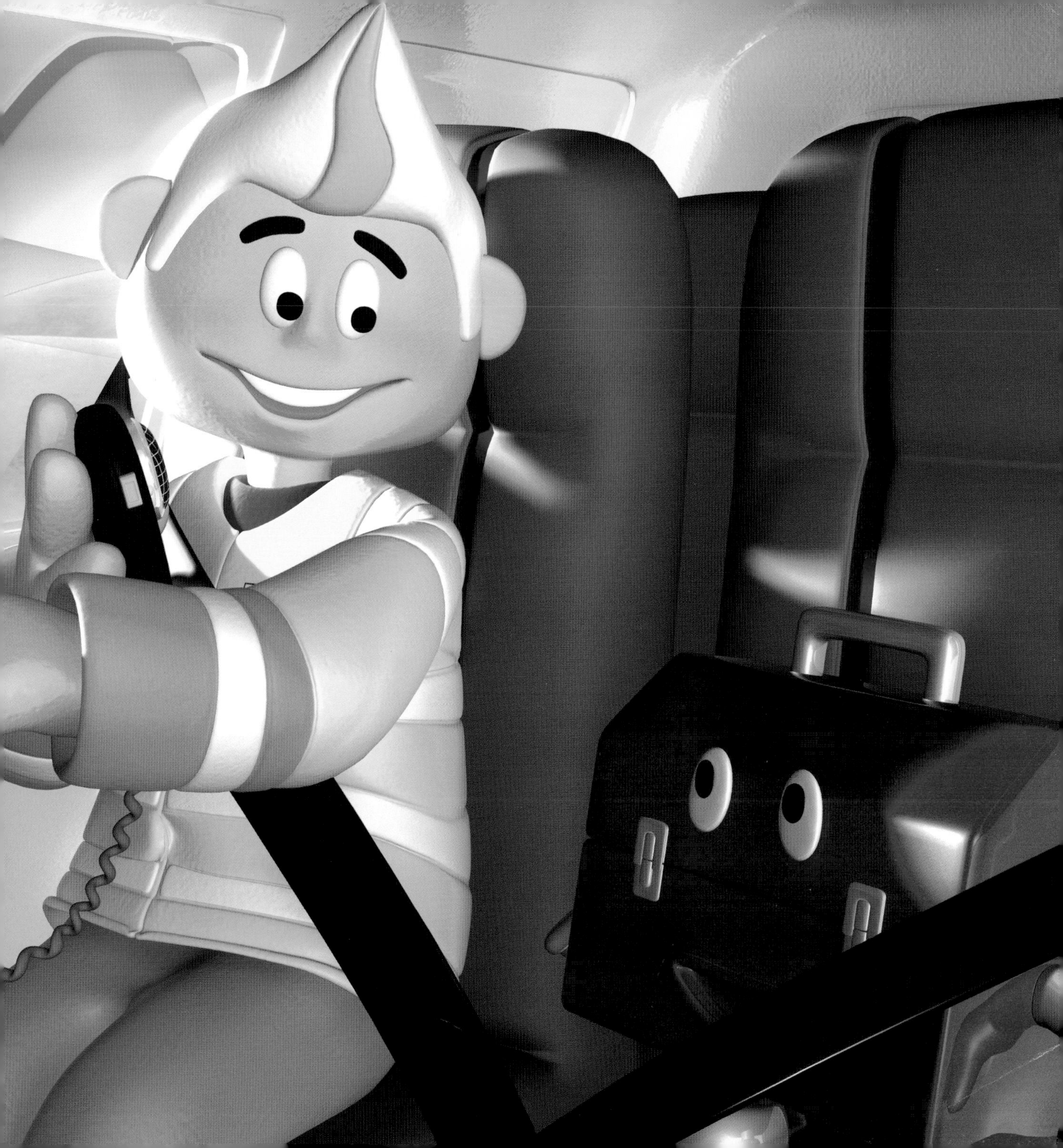

Following Rita's directions, Pete, Trevor and Stan soon came to a long queue of cars. At the end of the queue was Squad Car Sam.

"Oh dear," said Pete, when he saw that steam was coming from the engines of some of the cars. "It looks as if they've got too hot waiting in this queue."

"There's no way through," Pete said to Stan, "so you wait here while Trevor and I find Sergeant Dan."

AA

"Hello, my friends," boomed Sergeant Dan when he saw Pete and Trevor. "Thank goodness you've arrived so quickly. Cars have broken down all along this road. You'll never guess what's causing the hold up!"

Pete and Trevor looked at each other, then back at Sergeant Dan.

"Follow me," he said, "and I'll show you."

AA

Pete and Trevor gasped as they reached the front of the queue, but Sergeant Dan just shook his head.

They were faced by two enormous giraffes that stood in a cage on the back of a lorry. The lorry had stopped in front of a low bridge.

"So this is why there's such a long queue of traffic!" chuckled Pete.

The giraffe keeper ran up to Pete and Trevor.

"What shall I do? What shall I do?" he cried. "I'm taking these giraffes to their new home at the zoo, but the cage on the back of my lorry won't fit beneath the bridge. It's too tall!"

"Pete and Trevor to the rescue!" shouted Patrolman Pete and Trevor together.

Zoo
AA

Patrolman Pete ran back to Stan and returned with a rope in his hands.

"Use this rope to lead the giraffes from their cage," said Pete to the giraffe keeper, "while Sergeant Dan tells the car owners that they'll soon be on their way."

"Are you sure?" asked Sergeant Dan, looking concerned.

"Don't worry," replied Pete, "Trevor's got the right tools for the job!"

AA

Pete and Trevor began to take the cage apart, while the giraffe keeper looked on in amazement.

The giraffes had no idea of the problem they'd caused and kept bending their long necks down to lick Trevor with their wet tongues!

"Stop it!" Trevor giggled, after he'd been licked for the third time (even though it was quite nice on such a hot day!). Pete and Trevor soon had the cage in pieces and the lorry was ready to move.

Climbing into the lorry, Patrolman Pete drove it carefully beneath the bridge and parked it at the side of the road.

As Pete and Trevor rebuilt the cage, the keeper led the giraffes under the bridge. The giraffes had to bend their long necks because the bridge was so low, but they were soon safely on the other side.

"Now then," said Pete, "let's go and fix those cars!"

Pete and Trevor knew exactly what to do.

They started at the front of the queue and mended each and every car that wouldn't start.

Sergeant Dan began to direct the traffic beneath the bridge and soon all the cars had gone.

"Well done, Pete and Trevor," said Sergeant Dan, grinning at the hardworking patrolman and his trusty toolbox.

"I don't know how to thank you," said the giraffe keeper, "unless... wait a minute."

The keeper reached into his pocket and pulled out some tickets – tickets to visit the zoo!

"Would you like to come and see the giraffes in their new home?" he asked.

"Yes, please!" everyone replied.

It was time to go home after another busy day. Pete looked at the tickets the giraffe keeper had given him.

"I know," he said, "let's ask Rita if she'd like to visit the zoo with us. Without her, we wouldn't have had this adventure."

"What a good idea!" cried Trevor and Stan in agreement.

AA
AA

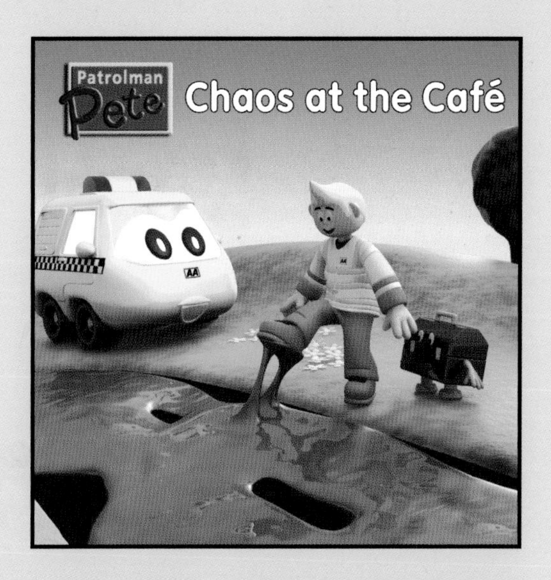

Collect all of the Patrolman Pete adventures!

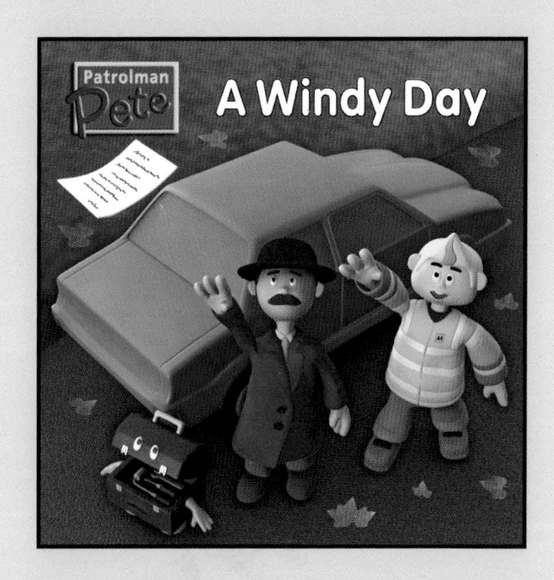